THIS BOOK BELONGS TO

Maia

Copyright © 2015

make believe ideas ltd

The Wilderness, Berkhamsted, Hertfordshire, HP4 2AZ, UK.

www.makebelieveideas.com

SNOW WHITE

Written by Helen Anderton

Illustrated by Stuart Lynch

make
believe
ideas

Reading together

This book is designed to be fun for children who are gaining confidence in their reading. They will enjoy and bene[fit] from some time discussing the story with an adult. Here are some ways you can help your child take those first steps in reading:

* Encourage your child to look at the pictures and talk about what is happening in the story.

* Help your child to find familiar words and sound out the letters in harder words.

* Ask your child to read and repeat each short sentence.

Look at rhymes

Many of the sentences in this book are simple rhymes. Encourage your child to recognise rhyming words. Try asking the following questions:

* What does this word say?

* Can you find a word that rhymes with it?

* Look at the ending of two words that rhyme. Are they spelt the same? For example, "wall" and "call", and "queen" and "mean".

Reading activities

The **What happens next?** activity encourages your child to retell the story and point to the mixed-up pictures in the right order.

The **Rhyming words** activity takes six words from the story and asks your child to read and find other words that rhyme with them.

The **Key words** pages provide practice with common words used in the context of the book. Read the sentences with your child and encourage him or her to make up more sentences using the key words listed around the border.

A **Picture dictionary** page asks children to focus closely on nine words from the story. Encourage your child to look carefully at each word, cover it with his or her hand, write it on a separate piece of paper, and finally, check it!

Do not complete all the activities at once – doing one each time you read will ensure that your child continues to enjoy the story and the time you are spending together. Have fun!

Snow White lives with a pretty queen,
who's cruel, unkind and just plain mean.
She talks to her mirror on the wall –
his name is Bill and here's his call:

'You gorgeous queen, you're fair, you're great!
    I'd love to take you on a date.
Says this mirror on the wall:
    the queen is fairest of them all!"

The queen just loves to wake each day
    and hear the things Bill has to say.
But then, one day, in sunny June,
    Bill decides to change his tune:

"You gorgeous queen, you're fair, it's true,
    but Snow White has grown more fair than you.
Says the mirror on the wall:
    Snow White is fairest of them all!"

The queen is cross. She stomps, then screams,
"Snow, you've ruined all my dreams!"

"You're banished now, go on, GET OUT!"
So Snow White doesn't hang about.

Snow runs and runs – she's terrified!
She needs to find a place to hide.
Then, seven dwarfs hop off a bus
and say, "Poor dear! Come live with us!"

STOP

BUS

13

Those dwarfs are such a happy bunch!
They let Snow stay and feed her lunch.
She tries to make their home looks nice.
She keeps it clean – and free of mice!

Back home, the queen works up a plot
and mixes poison in a pot.
She dips in apples, big and red.
"When Snow White bites one,
she'll be dead!"

Then, disguised in a cloak and hood,
the queen finds Snow White in the wood.

She gives her a red apple for lunch
and Snow falls down at the first crunch!

The dwarfs decide to place Snow White
 inside a case, and watch each night,
so her fair face they can remember.
 But then things change, for in September . . .

A prince sees Snow: "Wow, what a girl!
Hair like ebony, skin like pearl –
I have to kiss her, stand aside!"
One kiss and Snow opens her eyes!

The queen thinks it is safe at last
   to talk to Bill now Snow has passed.
"You gorgeous queen, you're fair, it's true,
   but Snow is still fairer than you!"

The queen replies, "I know you're wrong.
　　You must be broken; Snow is gone!"
She throws Bill out the castle door
　　and hears him crashing to the floor.

The queen is glad - she doesn't know
the fairest in the land is Snow.
Now, Snow White and the prince are free
to live together happily!

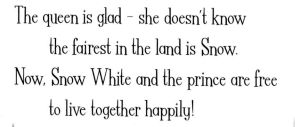

What happens next?

Some of the pictures from the story have been mixed up! Can you retell the story and point to each picture in the correct order?

Rhyming words

Read the words in the middle of each group and point to the other words that rhyme with them.

bean

mean

queen

trees

wood

apple

flow

snow

grow

house

crunch

mice

lunch

munch

prince

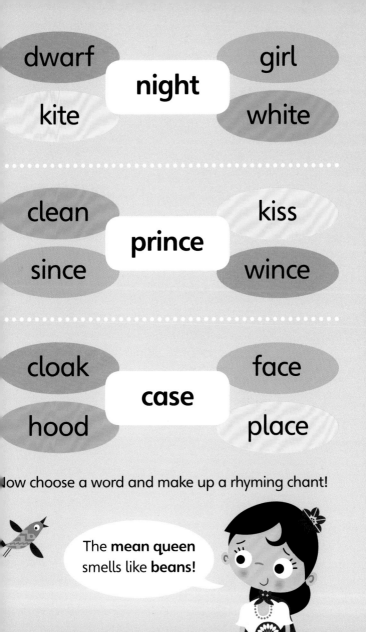

dwarf girl

night

kite white

clean kiss

prince

since wince

cloak face

case

hood place

Now choose a word and make up a rhyming chant!

The **mean queen** smells like **beans!**

Key words

These sentences use common words to describe the story. Read the sentences and then make up new sentences for the other words in the border.

The queen **asked** the mirror questions.

The mirror **said** Snow White was fairest.

Snow went **into** the woods.

The dwarfs hopped **off** a bus.

Snow kept the dwarfs' **house** clean.

like · asked

· his · but · said · into · all · we · called · are · up · o

Back at the palace, the queen was mad.

The queen **looked** different in a mask.

The queen gave Snow a **big** apple.

The prince asked Snow to marry **him**.

The queen didn't know **about** Snow and the prince.

the · and · to · not · looked · in · him · I · of · it · went · got · in · on · big · is · for

ouse · when · back · put · this · about · so · be ·

Picture dictionary

Look carefully at the pictures and the words.
Now cover the words, one at a time.
Can you remember how to write them?

apple

bus

castle

dwarf

hood

kiss

mirror

poison

wood